DATE DUE

DEC 2 6 2011			

CALICO ILLUSTRATED CLASSICS

Sir Arthur Conan Doyle's

Sherlock Holmes and the Hound of the Baskervilles

ADAPTED BY: Jan Fields

ILLUSTRATED BY: Antonio Javier Caparo

magic
wagon

visit us at www.abdopublishing.com

Published by Magic Wagon, a division of the ABDO Group,
8000 West 78th Street, Edina, Minnesota 55439. Copyright
© 2011 by Abdo Consulting Group, Inc. International copyrights
reserved in all countries. All rights reserved. No part of this
book may be reproduced in any form without written permission
from the publisher.

Calico Chapter Books™ is a trademark and logo of Magic Wagon.

Printed in the United States of America, Melrose Park, Illinois.
102010
012011

Original text by Sir Arthur Conan Doyle
Adapted by Jan Fields
Illustrated by Antonio Javier Caparo
Edited by Stephanie Hedlund and Rochelle Baltzer
Cover and interior design by Abbey Fitzgerald

Library of Congress Cataloging-in-Publication Data

Fields, Jan.
  Sherlock Holmes and the hound of the Baskervilles / Sir Arthur
Conan Doyle ; adapted by Jan Fields ; illustrated by Antonio Javier
Caparo.
     p. cm. -- (Calico illustrated classics)
  ISBN 978-1-61641-109-1
  [1. Dogs--Fiction. 2. Dartmoor (England)--History--20th century--
Fiction. 3. Great Britain--History--Edward VII, 1901-1910--Fiction.
4. Mystery and detective stories.] I. Caparo, Antonio Javier, ill. II.
Doyle, Arthur Conan, Sir, 1859-1930. The hound of the Baskervilles.
III. Title.
  PZ7.F479177Sh 2011
  [Fic]--dc22
                                          2010031011

Table of Contents

CHAPTER 1

Mr. Sherlock Holmes

I stood near the fire examining the walking stick our visitor had left the night before. Just under the uneven, round head of the stick, a silver band circled the fine wood. The engraving on the band read, "To James Mortimer, M.R.C.S. From his friends of the C.C.H. 1884."

"Well, Watson, what do you make if it?" asked Mr. Sherlock Holmes. Holmes sat with his back to me at the breakfast table. I had made no sound picking up the stick.

"How did you do that?" I demanded.

"With the help of a well-polished silver coffee pot," he said. "But do tell me what you have concluded from your examination of the stick. We missed the owner's visit, so it will be interesting to see what we can learn from what he left behind."

"I think," I said carefully, "Dr. Mortimer is an elderly country doctor who does a great deal of his visiting on foot. The stick is worn. The doctor is well thought of, since this stick was given as a mark of appreciation."

"Perfectly sound!" Holmes said.

Warming to my topic, I added, "I believe he has given some medical help to a hunt club, since the stick was given by the C.C.H. I believe we will learn that the *H* is for Hunt."

"Watson, you excel yourself," Holmes said as he pushed back his chair. "You have the remarkable ability to inspire genius, and I am in your debt."

I was proud to have mastered his system of deduction. Holmes rose and carried the cane to the window in order to look it over through his magnifying glass.

"Interesting, though elementary," he said as he settled in his favorite corner of the settee.

"Oh, did something escape me?" I asked.

"I am afraid, my dear Watson, that when I said you inspire genius, I meant that your mistakes help guide me toward the truth. Though this man is certainly a country doctor who walks a great deal."

"Then I was right."

"To that extent," he said. "Since he is a medical man, the stick was almost certainly given to him by the Charing Cross Hospital or C.C.H. Now what does that suggest?"

"That he practiced in town before moving to the country."

"Certainly that, but we can assume the stick was likely awarded at the time of the moving to a country practice. Now, since a celebrated doctor or administrator rarely moves from a thriving position to the country, we might assume this was upon his moving from a position of senior student to his own practice."

I nodded tentatively.

"Thus your elderly country doctor transforms into a young man, under thirty. He is absent-minded and has a beloved dog that is larger than a terrier but smaller than a mastiff."

At this, Holmes leaned back and gazed at the ceiling. Since the doctor had left his card, I pulled out a medical directory and looked up his name. It showed that he was all the things Holmes said, though I still could see no reason to deduce that he had a dog and mentioned as much.

"The dog has carried the stick," Holmes said. "The marks are clear on the wood. Thus, the dog must be large enough to bear a heavy stick, and we can see by the bite width that it could not be a beast as large as a mastiff. In fact, it is a curly-haired spaniel!"

"Now, how could you possibly know that?" I asked.

"I see him on our doorstep with his owner. Now, let us see what Dr. James Mortimer, the man of science, asks of Sherlock Holmes, the specialist in crime. Come in!"

The man who entered was very tall and thin with a long nose like a beak. His gray eyes were closely set and sparkled brightly behind a pair of gold-rimmed glasses. His frock coat was dingy and his trousers were frayed. As soon as he spotted his stick in Holmes's hand, he ran toward it with an exclamation of joy.

"I am delighted that you found my stick," he said.

"A presentation, I see," Holmes said.

"Yes, from friends at Charing Cross on the occasion of my marriage."

"Oh?" Holmes said, shaking his head. I nearly smiled to see him proved wrong in a small deduction.

"Yes sir, I married and so left the hospital to begin a consulting practice and make a home of my own. I presume that I am addressing Mr. Sherlock Holmes and this would be . . ." He looked at me then.

"This is my friend Dr. Watson."

"Glad to meet you, sir," he said with enthusiasm. "I've heard your name mentioned in connection with Mr. Holmes."

Holmes invited the doctor to sit and asked why he had come.

"I am suddenly confronted with a most serious problem, and as you are the second highest expert in Europe—"

"Indeed, sir! May I inquire who has the honor to be the first?" Holmes asked with some temper.

"To the man of precisely scientific mind, the work of Monsieur Bertillon must always appeal strongly."

"Then perhaps you should consult him!"

"But my problem is more practical than scientific, and in practical affairs, you stand alone. I trust I have not accidentally . . ."

"Just a little," Holmes said. "Perhaps it would be best if you explained your problem."

The Curse of the Baskervilles

"I have something I wish to read to you," Dr. Mortimer said.

"Something from the early-eighteenth-century manuscript in your pocket?" Holmes asked.

The doctor looked startled. "How do you know its age?"

"I see an inch or two of it above the line of your pocket. I would be a poor expert if I could not give the date of a document within a decade or two after seeing it for several minutes," Holmes said. "I put the date at 1730."

"The exact date is 1742." Dr. Mortimer drew it from his pocket. "This family paper was given to me several months ago by Sir

Charles Baskerville. He was my friend and my patient. His tragic death created quite a stir in Devonshire. My friend was an unimaginative, practical man, but he took the words of this document very seriously. It is the legend of the Baskerville family."

Holmes stretched the document out over his knees. I looked over his shoulder at the yellow paper and the faded ink.

"But surely you wish to consult with me over something more modern and practical?" Holmes asked.

"Most modern and practical," the doctor agreed. "It is a matter that must be decided in the next twenty-four hours. But this manuscript is related. May I read it to you?"

Holmes leaned back, placed his fingertips together, and closed his eyes. Dr. Mortimer lifted the manuscript to the best light and read in a high, crackling voice.

The manuscript told the tale of a demonic creature known as the "Hound of the Baskervilles." The story seemed to be mostly a warning to live a life of kindness to their neighbors. For a curse loomed over the family should any repeat the evildoing of their distant ancestor.

During the mid-1600s, the manor of the Baskervilles was held by a cruel man named Hugo Baskerville. Hugo became obsessed with the daughter of a local farmer, who had lands near the Baskerville estate, but she would have nothing to do with Hugo.

One night, Hugo rode to the farm with six of his wicked companions and kidnapped the young woman. They brought her to Baskerville Hall and locked her in an upstairs room. Then the men went downstairs to celebrate.

The young woman climbed out of the narrow window and scrambled down the thick ivy that covered the walls. Then she began the three-hour trek across the moor to reach her home.

After she had escaped, Hugo carried a plate of food up to his prisoner only to discover her gone. He ran down the stairs and demanded his friends help him recapture the young woman.

One of the men suggested Hugo set the hounds on her, so he did. Then he rode after them to find his prisoner. Hugo whipped his horse so fiercely that he soon rode far ahead of his friends.

When his companions had ridden a mile or two, they passed a night shepherd on the moor. The shepherd trembled with fear but admitted he had seen the young woman chased by hounds.

"But I have seen more than that," the terrified man cried. "Hugo Baskerville passed me on a black mare. Behind him ran an evil hound more horrible than anything I have ever seen."

The men scoffed at the shepherd but redoubled their efforts to catch up to Hugo. They feared what he would do when he finally reached the young woman.

Finally they came upon Hugo's hounds, slinking back toward them with hackles raised. Now the riders continued slowly, frightened to face whatever could make a pack of hounds shiver and whine.

They reached a clear spot and halted. Only the bravest was willing to creep close to the shadowy things that lay ahead. The moon shone brightly upon the clearing, and in the center the young woman's body lay in a crumpled heap. She had died from fear and exhaustion.

Near her lay Hugo Baskerville. A great black beast stood over him, its jaws dripping blood. It was larger than any hound they had ever seen. The monster looked up at them with blazing eyes, and the men fled for dear life.

Finally, the document warned that if any Baskerville should embrace a life of cruelty and selfishness like Hugo, the hound would come back for them.

When Dr. Mortimer finished reading, he pushed his spectacles up on his forehead. Holmes yawned.

"That would be of great interest to a collector of fairy tales," he said.

Then Dr. Mortimer pulled a folded newspaper from his pocket. "Now I would like to read this from the *Devon County Chronicle*, May 14 of this year."

The notice told of the death by heart attack of Sir Charles Baskerville. The reporter asserted that no foul play was suspected in the old man's death. The only odd things about the case were that Sir Charles was found lying dead outside the Hall with his face so contorted by strong emotion that he was difficult to identify.

The old man's footprints showed that he had been out walking, though the last portion of the walk seemed to have been made by walking on his toes. Finally, the reporter noted that an heir would soon be arriving from the United States to live in the Hall.

When Dr. Mortimer folded up the newspaper, Holmes said, "I must thank you for calling my attention to a case that certainly presents some features of interest. I assume you have more information than can be found in the account."

"I do," Dr. Mortimer said, "and I confide it only so I can get your advice. I have told no one else. Sir Charles was not well, so I attended him often. We became good friends. He was convinced a dreadful fate hung over his family and often asked me if I had heard the baying of a hound on the moor."

The doctor crossed the room to stare out the window as he remembered. "One night as we were riding together, an animal crossed our path. I assumed it was a black calf, but it clearly terrified Sir Charles. He grew so alarmed that I feared for his heart. I convinced him that he should leave for London to rest his nerves. He agreed but died the night before he was set to leave."

"And do you have any reason to wonder about the death?" I asked.

"Only one. When I examined the body, I found footprints in the soil a short distance away. They were the prints of a gigantic hound!"

CHAPTER 3

The Problem

At these words, a shudder passed through me. The doctor's voice had risen with emotion. Holmes leaned forward and his eyes had the hard, dry glitter of keen interest.

"You saw this?" he asked.

"As clearly as I see you."

"And you said nothing?"

"What was the use? The marks were some twenty yards from the body. I don't suppose I would have paid them any notice had I not known Sir Charles's fear of the legend."

"Did the prints approach the body?" Holmes asked.

"No. But the ground would not have taken prints well."

"What kind of night was it?"

"Damp and raw," Dr. Mortimer said. "But it was not actually raining."

"Tell me about the spot where he was found."

"There are two lines of an old yew hedge, twelve feet high and too thick to pass through. An eight-foot-wide walk runs down the center with a wicket gate that passes through the yews on one side. The gate leads to the moor."

"Can anyone enter the hedge from any point other than the moor gate or the house?" Holmes asked.

The doctor nodded. "There is an exit through a summer house at the far end."

"Was the moor gate closed?"

"Closed and padlocked. Sir Charles lay about fifty yards from the summer house, though he must have stood near the moor gate at least five or ten minutes. I found ash there from his cigar. His were the only footprints other than those of the dog."

Holmes leaped up and began to pace. "If only I could have been there to examine the fresh scene. You should have called me then!"

"The cause of death was very clear. Sir Charles died of a heart attack. His heart condition was severe and well known." The doctor hesitated then, dropped his eyes to the floor. "Also, the only other reason he might have died would have been supernatural, and you can imagine how little I want to give weight to that idea."

"But you believe it to be the curse?" Holmes asked.

The doctor shook his head. "No, but I do not disbelieve it as much as I would like. There have been reports of a huge hound on the moor. A creature that glows."

"I do not deal in the supernatural," Holmes said. "If you believe the creature is demonic, why do you seek me out?"

"I seek advice as to what I should do with Sir Henry Baskerville," the doctor said. "He arrives at the Waterloo Station in an hour and a quarter. He is the last heir, and I am not certain he should go to the manor. If he met the same fate, I would feel responsible."

"If the young man is under a demonic curse," Holmes said mildly, "could it not find him in London or even in the United States? I would imagine the devil is not bound to Devonshire."

The doctor frowned at Holmes's light tone. "What would you recommend?"

"Proceed to the station to meet Sir Henry Baskerville. Say nothing to him about the matter but bring him here at ten o'clock tomorrow."

"I will do so." The doctor scribbled the appointment on his shirt cuff and hurried to collect his dog, who was scratching at the door. Holmes caught him just before he left to ask if anyone had reported sightings of the demonic hound after the death of Sir Charles.

"I have not heard of any," the doctor said.

Holmes bid him good morning and returned to his settee to think. He then sent me on my way until evening so he might ponder the case alone in deep quiet. I spent the day at my club and did not return until nearly nine o'clock that evening.

"Did you have a good day at your club?" Holmes asked, then laughed at my bewildered expression. "You have been gone all day. The weather is muddy and showery but your boots still shine, so clearly you've been indoors."

"It is rather obvious," I said.

"The world is full of obvious things that no one notices," Holmes said. "I have been studying a map of the moor."

"It must be a wild place," I said.

"It is a worthy setting," Holmes leaned forward. "We have two questions at the onset. Was a crime committed? And if there was a crime, how was it committed? Have you been thinking about the case?"

"Yes," I said.

"What do you make of the change in Sir Charles's footprints?"

"Mortimer said the man had walked on tiptoe down part of the alley."

Holmes snorted. "He only repeated what someone said at the inquest. Why would a man walk on tiptoe down an alley? He was running, Watson. He was running so desperately that he burst his heart and fell down dead."

"Running from what?"

"That is the problem," Holmes said. "Also, it was a wet evening. Why would an elderly man with serious medical problems stand around outside on such a night?"

"He had a habit of a nightly walk," I reminded him.

"Walk, yes. But he stood for some minutes at the gate. Why? Who was he waiting for? According to Dr. Mortimer, the old man was terrified of the moor and the beast he believed lived there. Why would he stand there? The thing takes shape. We need only seek out more pieces. Tomorrow we will hear from Sir Henry Baskerville."

Sir Henry Baskerville

Holmes waited in his dressing gown for our clients. The clock had just struck ten when Dr. Mortimer arrived with the young baronet. Sir Henry Baskerville was a short, dark-eyed man of about thirty. He had a sturdy build and the weather-beaten look of someone who had spent most of his time in the open air.

"The strange thing is that if my friend here had not suggested coming to see you this morning, I would have come anyway," Sir Henry said. "I understand you're good with puzzles, and I've had a troubling one this morning."

Holmes leaned forward, his eyes keen with interest.

"I expect it is a joke," Sir Henry said. "I received this letter this morning."

He laid an envelope upon the table, and we all bent over it. It looked common enough. The address was printed in rough characters and read, "Sir Henry Baskerville, Northumberland Hotel." The postmark read "Charing Cross" and showed it had been sent the previous evening.

"Who knew that you would be staying at the Northumberland Hotel?" asked Holmes, glancing keenly across at our visitor.

"I only decided after I met Dr. Mortimer," he said, running his hand through his black hair. "Dr. Mortimer wasn't even staying there. He was staying with a friend."

"Someone seems to be deeply interested in your movements." Holmes took a half sheet of cheap paper from the envelope. He opened the paper and spread it flat on the table. Across the paper a single sentence was formed from pasting words onto the paper.

The message read: As you value your life or your sanity keep away from the moor.

"Someone might be warning you away from the curse," Holmes said.

"Why do I get the feeling that you gentlemen know a great deal more than I do about my own affairs?" Sir Henry asked sharply.

"We shall certainly share our knowledge," Holmes said. "But first, have you yesterday's *Times*, Watson?"

Holmes glanced swiftly over the pages, running his eyes up and down the columns. Then he pointed out the section from which the words in the message had been clipped.

"Notice that the word 'moor' is handwritten in the note. This is because it doesn't occur in any of the articles in this particular issue," Holmes announced.

"By thunder, you're right! Well, if that isn't smart!" cried Sir Henry.

"Really, Mr. Holmes, this exceeds anything I could have imagined," Dr. Mortimer said, gazing at my friend in amazement. "How did you do it?"

"The detection of different typefaces is one of the most elementary branches of knowledge to an expert in crime. Once I recognized the typeface, finding the article was simple, as we know it was likely to come from last night's paper. Someone cut out these words with nail scissors and pasted it with gum."

"Can you tell anything else from this message, Mr. Holmes?" asked the young baronet.

"The *Times* is a paper which is seldom found in any hands but those of the highly educated. The words are not in an exact line, suggesting the person creating the note was upset or hurried. Did the writer fear an interruption? And from whom?"

"Now we are entering guesswork," said Dr. Mortimer.

"No, this is the scientific use of the imagination, based on physical evidence. And it suggests that this was written in a hotel. The pen and the ink seem to have given the writer trouble. It is rare that anyone would encounter that in their home, but fairly common when using hotel stationery."

Holmes carefully examined the paper, holding it only an inch or two from his eyes. Then he set it down and asked Sir Henry if anything else unusual had happened.

"Well, I have lost one of my boots," Sir Henry said. "That is certainly unusual for me."

"My dear sir," Dr. Mortimer cried, "it is only mislaid. That is hardly a mystery."

"It might be," Holmes said. "Tell me how it came to be."

"I bought a pair of boots last night. I never had them on. They had never been polished, so I set them outside my door last night. There was only one in the morning. I could get no sense out of the chap who cleans them."

"It seems a singularly useless thing to steal," said Sherlock Holmes. "I confess that I share Dr. Mortimer's belief that it will not be long before the missing boot is found."

"And now I've shared my mystery," Sir Henry said. "I believe it is time you shared yours."

Dr. Mortimer drew his papers from his pocket and presented his case to Sir Henry as he had to us the day before. Sir Henry listened with the deepest attention and with an occasional exclamation of surprise.

"Well, I seem to have come into an interesting inheritance," Sir Henry said when the doctor finished. "I have certainly heard of the hound, as it is the pet story of our family. I've never taken it seriously before. And now we have the strange letter to make things even less clear."

"It seems to show that someone knows more than we do about what goes on upon the moor," said Dr. Mortimer.

"And," said Holmes, "that someone wishes to protect you, since they warn you of danger."

"Or they want to scare me away," said Sir Henry.

"Now we must decide whether or not you should go to Baskerville Hall," Holmes said.

"There is no devil or man who will prevent me from going to the home of my people. You may take that as my final answer." Sir Henry's dark brows lowered over his eyes and his face reddened as he spoke. "I'm heading back to my hotel now. Why don't you and Dr. Watson come round at lunch. I'll be able to tell you more clearly then how this thing strikes me."

We quickly agreed and the two men left to walk back to their hotel. We heard the steps of our visitors on the stairs and the bang of the front door. Then Holmes hurried after them. When we reached the street, Dr. Mortimer and Sir Henry had walked well ahead of us in the direction of Oxford Street.

"Shall I run on and stop them?" I asked.

"Not for all the world, my dear Watson. It is a very fine morning for a walk."

We followed the men at a leisurely pace. Suddenly Holmes gave a little cry of satisfaction. I followed his eager eyes and saw a hansom cab with a man inside. I was aware of a bushy black beard and a pair of piercing eyes turned upon us through the side window of the cab.

Instantly the trapdoor at the top flew open, something was screamed to the driver, and the cab flew madly off. Holmes dashed after it, but the cab was quickly out of sight.

"What a sad combination of bad luck and bad management," Holmes grumbled. "We knew someone was watching Baskerville. They must've followed him the first day, and I assumed they would today as well. I was expecting someone on foot. The cab surprised me, and I handled it poorly. At least I have the cab number. We can speak to the driver later."

We had been strolling slowly down Regent Street during this conversation. Dr. Mortimer and Sir Henry had long disappeared from in front of us.

Holmes turned into one of the district messenger offices, where he was greeted warmly by the manager. He asked the man for the use of one of his messenger boys. A lad of fourteen with a bright face soon stood gazing with great reverence at Holmes.

"Cartwright, there are twenty-three hotels in the immediate neighborhood of Charing Cross. I wish you to visit each of these in turn. I want you to search the wastepaper of yesterday and look for the center page of the *Times* that has holes cut in it with scissors. The odds are against your finding it, but I want you to look. Let me have a report by wire at Baker Street."

Holmes handed the lad some money and sent him on his way. Then we set about to pass the time until our next appointment.

CHAPTER
5

Three Broken Threads

When we arrived at the Northumberland Hotel, Holmes asked to look at the hotel register and the clerk agreed. Two people had checked in after Sir Henry Baskerville, but they were frequent visitors and the clerk knew them well.

As we walked upstairs together, Holmes said in a low voice, "We know now that the people interested in our friend are not staying at this hotel. That suggests they do not want Sir Henry to see them."

Just as I was going to ask him what that might mean to the investigation, we ran up against Sir Henry. His face was red and he clutched a worn black boot in one hand.

"They're playing with the wrong man at this hotel," he roared.

"Another boot problem?" Holmes asked.

"Yes, sir, and I mean to get to the bottom of it. I only have three pairs of boots in the world: the new brown, the old black, and the patent leathers I'm wearing. Last night someone made off with one of the brown boots. Today they've taken one of the black!"

As he spoke, a member of the hotel staff appeared. He assured Sir Henry that a search for his boots was in progress. Sir Henry grumbled a bit more and the employee dashed away.

"Sorry to trouble you," Sir Henry said.

"I think it is well worth troubling over," Holmes said. "This case of yours is very complex, with threads that seem to run in all directions. One of them will guide us to the truth."

We proceeded then to a pleasant luncheon in a private sitting room. Afterward, Holmes asked what Sir Henry had decided.

"To go to Baskerville Hall at the end of the week!" Sir Henry replied.

"I think your decision is a wise one," Holmes said. "We have evidence that you are being dogged here in London, where the culprit can vanish in crowds. In the country, he may stand out more clearly."

Then Holmes told our friends of the man who had followed them in the cab. He admitted he had failed to discover the man's identity.

"Dr. Mortimer, do you know anyone on Dartmoor with a black, full beard?"

"Only Barrymore. He is in charge of the Hall," Dr. Mortimer said.

"We had best learn if he made a trip to London," Holmes said.

"How?" Dr. Mortimer asked.

"I will send a telegraph to be presented into the hand of Mr. Barrymore and ask that you receive a return wire if the telegram cannot be delivered to him."

Holmes retrieved a telegraph form from a near table and printed the message: "Is all ready for Sir Henry?"

"Good plan," Baskerville said. "Who is this Barrymore anyhow?"

"The son of the old caretaker," Dr. Mortimer said. "His family has looked after the Hall for four generations. Sir Charles was very fond of them. He left them 500 pounds each in his will."

"If they could scare me off, they'd have a fine home and nothing to do," Baskerville said.

"Did they know of the provisions of the will?" Holmes asked.

"Oh yes, most everyone did," Dr. Mortimer said. "Sir Charles loved to talk about it. Though if you are suspicious of everyone who inherited, I should confess that I received 1,000 pounds myself."

"Indeed! And anyone else?" Holmes asked.

"Quite a few small sums to individuals and charities," Dr. Mortimer said. "The rest comes to Sir Henry. It will be about 740,000 pounds."

Holmes raised his eyebrows in surprise. "With so much money at stake, a man might well play a desperate game. Who would receive the money if something happened to Sir Henry?"

"Well, there was another brother," Dr. Mortimer said. "But Rodger Baskerville died unmarried in South America. The estate would fall to a distant cousin in Westmoreland. He's an elderly gentleman named James Desmond."

"Have you met Mr. Desmond?" Holmes asked.

"Yes, actually," the doctor said. "He is a very old man of simple tastes who wouldn't even accept a gift from Sir Charles."

Holmes said to Sir Henry, "I believe you must go to Devonshire, but not alone. I have in mind a man you can count on without hesitation. There is no better man to have at your side when you're in a tight place." Then he turned to me and laid his hand on my arm.

Before I could even answer, Sir Henry grabbed my hand and shook it hard. "That is kind of you, Dr. Watson," he said. "I'll never forget this."

I was touched by Holmes's statement of trust and eager for the adventure. Holmes assured me that he would join me as soon as he could. He added that I should not let Sir Henry out on the moor on his own under any circumstances.

And so I prepared to leave, but before the day of our departure, a curious thing occurred. Sir Henry found his new brown boot lying in the corner of his room. The older boot was never recovered. Baskerville also received a response to the telegraph Holmes sent. Barrymore was at the Hall.

Almost at the same time, we received a message from the young man who had searched for the newspaper from which the message had been cut. He had found no such newspaper in the rubbish of any of the hotels.

We also met with the cab driver who had driven the cab with the mysterious bearded passenger. The driver seemed quite proud to be questioned and told us that he knew exactly who his passenger was.

"When he paid me to drop him at the station," the cab driver said, "he said I'd been driving the famous Mr. Sherlock Holmes!"

When the cabman departed, Holmes turned with a shrug of his shoulders and a sad smile. "Our opponent has certainly sent a bold message. I've been checkmated in London. I wish you better luck in Devonshire."

CHAPTER 6

Baskerville Hall

Holmes drove with me to the station to leave with Sir Henry and Dr. Mortimer. He encouraged me to send detailed reports of any discussions between Sir Henry and his neighbors and anything else I might learn about the death of Sir Charles.

"There are only a few neighbors. I believe Dr. Mortimer to be completely honest. There is a butterfly expert nearby who lives with his sister. There is Mr. Frankland of Lafter Hall. And pay special attention to the Barrymore couple and the groom at the Hall."

"I will do my best," I said solemnly.

"We have no new events to report," Dr. Mortimer said when we met them on the platform. "I have kept a sharp eye out and no one has followed us."

Holmes cautioned Sir Henry to go nowhere alone. "Something horrible will befall you if you do. And remember especially to avoid the moor after dark."

When our train finally pulled out, I looked back at the platform. There, I saw the tall figure of Holmes standing motionless as he gazed after us.

Our journey was swift and pleasant. Sir Henry stared eagerly out of the window and cried aloud with delight as he recognized the familiar features of the Devon scenery.

"I've been over a good bit of the world," Sir Henry said. "But I have never seen a place that compares with Devonshire. I've never actually seen the Hall, though. It will be as new to me as it is to Dr. Watson."

"Ah," Dr. Mortimer said, pointing out of the window. "We've nearly reached the moor."

In the distance, a gray hill with a strange jagged summit contrasted with the rolling green surrounding us. Sir Henry sat for a long time with his eyes focused on it.

The train pulled up at a small wayside station and we all hurried off the train. Outside, a small wagon with a pair of stocky, short-legged horses was waiting. I was surprised to see two men in dark uniforms nearby, leaning upon short rifles. They glanced keenly at us as we passed to reach the wagon.

The coachman saluted Sir Henry and we were soon flying down the broad road. Rolling pastures curved upward on either side of us and old gabled houses peeped out from the thick, green hedges. At every turn, Sir Henry gave an exclamation of delight.

"What is this?" Dr. Mortimer cried as we rounded a curve. We saw a mounted soldier with his rifle ready as he watched the road.

Our driver half turned in his seat. "There's a convict escaped from Princetown, sir. He's been out three days now. The farmers here don't like it a bit."

"Who is he?" I asked.

"Selden, the Notting Hill murderer."

I knew that case. It had been a particularly brutal one. The man would have been executed, except the judge felt he wasn't quite sane. As this information sunk in, our wagon topped a hill. A cold wind swept down from it and set us shivering. Even Sir Henry fell silent and pulled his coat more tightly around him.

We looked down into a cuplike depression, patched with stunted oaks. Two high, narrow towers rose over the trees. The driver pointed with his whip. "Baskerville Hall."

A few minutes later, we reached the gates with weathered pillars on either side. Through the gateway, we passed into the avenue where old trees shot their branches in a tunnel over our heads.

"Did my uncle die here?" Sir Henry asked in a low voice.

"No," the doctor said. "The yew alley is on the other side."

The young heir glanced around with a frown. "This gloom is enough to scare any man. I'll have electric lights brought in, and you'll not know the place in six months.

The center of the hall was draped in ivy except where windows peered through. Two ancient towers stood on either side. And beyond them, modern wings of black granite stood, bare of ivy.

"Welcome, Sir Henry," a man's voice called. "Welcome to Baskerville Hall!"

A tall man had stepped from the porch, followed by a sturdy figure of a woman. They began to collect our bags as we said our farewells to Dr. Mortimer, who was eager to get home to his wife.

Sir Henry and I entered the Hall and found it lofty, with a huge fireplace where a log fire crackled and snapped. We stood by the fire to warm the chill we had picked up on our drive.

"It's just as I imagined it," Sir Henry said, his face bright again.

Just then, Barrymore returned from taking our luggage to our rooms. He was tall and handsome with a well-trimmed beard and pale features. He asked if we would like dinner and we replied enthusiastically.

"My wife and I will be happy to stay with you until you have made fresh arrangements for staff," Barrymore said. "When it is convenient for you, we plan to establish ourselves in some business."

"I will be sorry to see you go," Sir Henry said. "Your family has been with us for several generations, I believe."

Barrymore nodded. "To tell the truth, we were both very attached to Sir Charles. His death makes these surroundings painful for us. I fear we shall never be easy in our minds at Baskerville Hall."

We ate dinner in a dark, gloomy dining room and then retired for the night. I tossed restlessly, thinking about the details of the day. Then suddenly, I was jolted completely awake by the sound of a woman sobbing in uncontrollable sorrow. The sound stopped just as suddenly, and though I listened, I heard only the rustle of the ivy on the outside walls.

The Stapletons of Merripit House

The fresh beauty of the following morning brightened both our moods and the gloom of the dining room. Sunlight flooded in through the high windows. The dark paneling glowed like bronze in the golden rays.

"Now that I am fresh and well, all is cheerful once more," Sir Henry said.

"Did you happen to hear a woman sobbing in the night?" I asked.

"That is curious," he answered. "I heard something of the sort, but since the sound was not repeated, I assumed it was my imagination."

"I heard it distinctly," I said.

Sir Henry decided this was a mystery we

should solve at once. He rang for Barrymore, who assured him that only two women lived in the house. The scullery maid's room was too far from ours for the sound to carry. And he was certain his own wife had not been crying.

Later I met Mrs. Barrymore in the long corridor, where the sun shone full on her face. Her eyes were red and swollen. Clearly she had been crying. Why would Barrymore lie about such a thing?

I decided to check up on Barrymore's alibi for the events in London. I walked into the village and checked with the Grimpen postmaster. The telegraph had not been delivered directly to Barrymore's hand. In fact, the boy who carried the message had not seen Barrymore at all.

"He was up in the loft at the time," the message carrier said. "I gave it to Mrs. Barrymore and she promised to deliver it at once."

I walked back from the postmaster, pondering what this new information might mean. I was interrupted in these thoughts by the sound of running feet behind me. A voice called out my name. I turned to see a small stranger in a gray suit running toward me with a green butterfly net in one hand.

"Excuse me," he puffed when he reached me. "I am Stapleton of Merripit House. Perhaps our mutual friend Mortimer mentioned me?"

"I would have known you from your net," I said. "I heard you were an expert on butterflies and moths. How did you know me?"

"I was calling on Dr. Mortimer just now, and he pointed you out as you passed," the small man said. "I trust that Sir Henry is well?"

"Very well, thank you."

"Excellent!" He beamed at me. "We were all so afraid he wouldn't come after the sad death of Sir Charles. The peasants are all convinced he was killed by the hound. I do wonder at the part it may have played, if only in Sir Charles's imagination."

"How is that?"

"His nerves were so worked up from the stories that the sight of any dog might have brought on an attack," Stapleton said. "I knew his heart was weak."

"You think Sir Charles ran from a dog and died?" I asked.

"It seems logical," he answered. "What does Mr. Sherlock Holmes think?"

My surprise must have shown on my face because he then said, "Everyone has read your retelling of cases solved by Mr. Sherlock Holmes. We assumed you were here for the case of Sir Charles."

"I am merely here to visit with my friend, Sir Henry," I said.

"Of course," he said, looking at me slyly.

We had come to a point where a narrow, grassy path struck off from the road to wind through the moor. "Merripit House lies up this moor path. Would you come and meet my sister?"

As Sherlock had told me to report on the locals, I agreed. We walked a bit as Stapleton talked about his love of the moor.

"You cannot think the secrets it contains," Stapleton proclaimed. "It is so vast and so barren and so mysterious." He pointed across at a great plain to the north with a hill breaking out of it. "What do you think of that?"

"It looks like a good place for a gallop!"

"Some have thought so and paid heavily for their mistake," he said. "It is the Grimpen Mire. A false step will suck you down into a bog hole. Look there, a moor pony is caught!"

Something brown was rolling and tossing among the tufts of tall grasses. Then a long, writhing neck shot upward and a dreadful cry echoed over the moor. The sound made ice shoot up my back.

"The mire has him," Stapleton said calmly. "That's a bad place and best avoided. I have only just learned to make my way through it."

"Perhaps I will try," I said.

Stapleton's eyes widened in shock. "You must not. I would not want your death on my head for pointing out the place."

I might have argued the point if we were not interrupted by a sad moan that swept over the moor. "What was that?" I asked.

"The peasants say it's the Hound of the Baskervilles," Stapleton said. "But I expect it's a moor bird or the wind in the hollows. It can echo strangely among those." He pointed toward the steep slope beyond us. On the hillside I could see at least twenty circular rings of stone. I asked what the odd structures were.

"Prehistoric homes," Stapleton answered. "If you had the curiosity to examine them, you could see the ancient hearths and beds left behind by Neolithic man."

Then suddenly Stapleton turned and launched across the moor in pursuit of a small butterfly. I watched him hop and race, waving his net. The sound of light footsteps came up behind me and I turned to see a tall, beautiful young woman with dark, eager eyes.

"Go back," she said fiercely to me. "Go straight back to London, instantly."

I could only stare in surprise. "Why?" I asked.

"I cannot explain," she said in her low, anxious voice. "But go and never set foot upon the moor again. Start tonight!" Then she looked sharply across the moor. "Hush, my brother is coming. Not a word of what I said."

When Stapleton was in earshot, she added, "We are very rich in orchids on the moor, though you are rather late to see the beauties of the place."

Stapleton was flushed from his run. He spoke to the young woman sharply. "Hello Beryl."

"You look very hot," she said mildly.

"Yes, I was chasing a Cyclopides but I missed him," he said. "I see you have introduced yourself."

"Yes, I was telling Sir Henry about the local flowers," she said.

"No, no," I said. "I am only a humble commoner, though a friend to Sir Henry. My name is Dr. Watson."

"Oh, how silly of me," she said, flushing deeply. "Then you would have no interest in the changing plants of the moor. Are you coming to see Merripit House?"

I went on with them, still a bit bewildered by the oddness of my day so far. Theirs was a bleak moorland house with wind-stunted trees around it. It gave the whole place a sad look.

"I was a schoolmaster in the north country until a serious illness broke out in the school. I never quite recovered from the shock of students dying," Stapleton said. "So I came here where I could pursue my interest in nature, and my sister came along. We are very happy here, aren't we, Beryl?"

"Quite happy," she said in a tone that held no real warmth.

"It would seem a dull place for a young woman," I said.

"I am never bored," she said in the same tone.

"We keep busy," Stapleton assured me. "I'm thinking we'll come this afternoon to visit Sir Henry. Do you think he would mind?"

"I believe he would enjoy it," I said, and I left soon after. I had gone only a short way from the house when Stapleton's sister rushed out after me. She begged me to forget all about the silly things she had said.

"I can hardly forget them," I said. "Should I be worried for my friend?"

"It is a woman's whim only," she said, adding a false laugh. "Though if you have power with Sir Henry, you might use it to take him back to London. The moor can be an unhealthy place. I must go now. My brother doesn't like me to be silly."

She turned and fled back to the house, leaving me staring after her.

The First Report of Dr. Watson

Baskerville Hall, October 13th

My Dear Holmes,

My last report was days ago because so little has happened. There is strong reason to believe the escaped convict has gotten away. With nothing to eat, he would not long remain on the moor without capture, even though there are plenty of places to hide.

I admit we sleep easier knowing he must be gone. We were deeply concerned about the Stapletons. The brother is a small man and their only hired man is quite elderly. Sir Henry offered to send his groom, Perkins, to stay with them, but Stapleton would not hear of it.

Stapleton showed us the very spot where wicked Hugo met his death in the legend. Sir Henry asked many questions. I could plainly see that both men tend to believe this old legend. Stapleton even told a story of another family afflicted by a similar curse that eventually wiped out every member.

It was upon returning from that walk that Sir Henry met Miss Stapleton for the first time. He has talked of her constantly since and hardly a day has passed without our seeing the brother and sister. They are to dine with us tonight.

A match between the baronet and Miss Stapleton would seem ideal, but it's clear her brother does not share that view. I have seen him glare at Sir Henry several times when the baronet and Miss Stapleton have been in conversation. He has also prevented them from having any moments alone. I expect he is afraid he'll be left quite alone if his sister marries.

If Stapleton should allow his sister time alone with Sir Henry, it will be difficult for me to remain at his side every moment. I would quickly become quite an unpopular companion when two young people want to be alone.

Dr. Mortimer lunched with us on Thursday along with the Stapletons. He took us all to the yew alley to show us exactly how everything occurred on that fatal night. The path through the yews is long and dismal. At the far end is a ruined summer house. Halfway down is the white, wooden moor gate, where the old gentleman left his cigar ash.

I tried to picture all that had occurred. As the old man stood near the gate, he saw something racing toward him across the moor. In terror, he ran toward the summerhouse instead of the Hall. He ran until he died of fear and exhaustion. But what chased him? A sheepdog of the moor? Or a silent demon hound? It was all dim and vague, but there is the dark shadow of crime behind it.

I have met the other neighbor since last I reported. Mr. Frankland of Lafter Hall lives some four miles south of us. He is elderly and red-faced. His passion is lawsuits. He fights for the mere pleasure of fighting and takes suit against his neighbors for the oddest things.

He is said to have about seven lawsuits upon his hands at present. Other than this passion for suing people, he seems good-natured. He is also something of an amateur astronomer and has a very fine telescope. He's been using it to watch the moor for the escaped convict, but no luck so far.

He did hint that he may have evidence for a new lawsuit though. I have to admit, he's a nice speck of comic relief.

Finally, I need to tell you about the Barrymores. When I told Sir Henry about the telegram, he decided to have a talk with Barrymore immediately. He asked him if he had received the telegram. Barrymore said he had.

"Did the boy give it to you directly?" Sir Henry asked.

"No," Barrymore said after a thoughtful pause. "I was in the box-room. My wife gave it to me."

"Did you answer it yourself?"

"No, I wasn't finished with my chore. I told my wife to answer, but I'm certain she wrote down exactly what I said."

He then asked if he had done something to cause Sir Henry to distrust him. Sir Henry assured him that he was completely comfortable with Barrymore's service. Then to mollify any hurt feelings, he gave the servant a considerable part of his old wardrobe, since new clothes had arrived from London.

Mrs. Barrymore interests me. She seems an unemotional person, but I have seen traces of tears several times. Then an adventure last night left me very suspicious.

Last night, I was awakened by a stealthy step passing my door. I rose and peeped out. A man wearing a shirt and trousers but no shoes was walking softly, carrying a candle. His height told me that it was Barrymore.

I waited until he had passed out of sight around a corner, then I followed him. He entered one of the empty rooms in a farther corridor. These rooms are unfurnished and unoccupied. The light of his candle shone steady as if he were standing motionless. I crept to the doorway and peeked in.

Barrymore crouched at the window with his candle held against the glass. He stared out at the moor. Then he groaned and put out the light. I hurried back to my room, and he passed soon after with the same soft footsteps. I've told Sir Henry about it. We have a plan.

The Second Report of Dr. Watson

Baskerville Hall, October 15th

My Dear Holmes,

Events are now crowding thick and fast upon us. After following Barrymore in the night, I examined the unfinished room by daylight. The window he peered through gives the closest view of the moor of all the windows in the Hall.

I felt I had to share what I had seen with Sir Henry.

"I knew Barrymore walked about nights," he said. "I've heard his footsteps."

"Perhaps he pays a visit to that particular window each time," I said.

"We should follow him and see what he is after." He looked thoughtful for a moment, then added, "I wonder what Mr. Holmes would do if he were here."

"I believe he would do exactly as you suggest," I said.

"Then we will sit up in my room tonight until Barrymore passes and then follow."

After our conversation, Sir Henry put on his hat to go out and I did the same. "Are you coming, Watson?"

"I promised Holmes not to leave you alone," I said.

He put his hand upon my shoulder with a pleasant smile. "But there are circumstances Holmes could not have foreseen. I plan different company on the moor today."

At that, he picked up his cane and was gone. I could not rest after having let him go. If he were harmed because I did not accompany him, I would never forgive myself. So, I set off at once in the direction of Merripit House.

I did not see Sir Henry until I climbed the hill at the point where the moor path branches off. Sir Henry and Miss Stapleton walked slowly on the moor path.

I stood behind the rocks, watching and debating what I should do. I was too far away to be much use if sudden danger came upon him, but I didn't know what else I could do. My eye was drawn to a wisp of green, and I turned to see Stapleton with his butterfly net. He was clearly moving in the direction of Sir Henry and his sister.

Sir Henry put his arm around the lady, but she seemed to strain away from him. Then they sprang apart and turned around. Stapleton ran toward them, clearly shouting. He seemed to be furious and waved his hands wildly. Finally he signaled his sister with a jerk of his head and stomped away with her walking beside him.

The baronet turned back to the Hall glumly. Soon we met, and he told me that Stapleton had acted wild with fury.

"Can you think of any reason someone would think I would be a bad husband for Miss Stapleton?" he asked.

"I should say not," I assured him. "Did he say that?"

"He said that and a good bit more," he replied. "From the first moment I saw her, I've felt she was made for me. And she's happy with me, though she won't speak of it. She insists I should leave the moor. I was going to tell her today that I would leave if she would leave with me, but her brother cut our discussion short."

Stapleton came to the Hall a few hours later and apologized to Sir Henry for his rudeness. He said his sister was everything in his life and the thought of losing her was terrible.

"He asked if I would give him three months to grow used to the idea of being alone," Sir Henry told me. "He promised he would withdraw all opposition if I would give him that time to adjust."

I do think Stapleton's behavior was horribly selfish, but the mystery seems to be solved.

Now I will tell of the second mystery solved: the Barrymores.

Sir Henry and I sat in his dark room as the hours crawled by slowly. We had almost given up when we both heard a creak in the passage.

The soft steps passed the door and we set out in pursuit. We followed along until we came into the other wing and caught a glimpse of the tall, black-bearded figure of Barrymore entering the same room as before.

We peeked in the door and found him crouched at the window. The baronet is a direct man, so he simply walked into the room and said, "What are you doing here, Barrymore?"

"Nothing, sir." The man was so upset he could barely speak. Shadows leaped against the wall because the candle in his hand shook so. "I check on the windows at night to be certain they are fastened."

"Look here," Sir Henry said sternly, "tell the truth. Why were you at that window specifically?"

"I was doing no harm, sir," Barrymore said. "I was holding a candle to the window. I cannot say why."

"It was a signal," I said. I took the candle and held it to the window. I stared across the black bank of the trees and the moor beyond. I cried out when a tiny pinpoint of yellow light glowed steadily in the darkness. "There, an answering signal."

"No, no, sir," Barrymore cried. "It is nothing."

"If you will not speak honestly, then you will leave my employ in disgrace!" Sir Henry said. "I cannot believe that you would plot against me."

"No, sir," a female voice cried from behind us. "Not against you."

We turned to face Mrs. Barrymore. "My brother is starving on the moor," she cried. "We cannot let him perish at our very gates. We signal when food is ready and he signals back to show where to take it."

Her brother was Selden, the escaped convict. For all that he was an evil man, his older sister

loved him. In her heart, he was always the curly-headed little boy of her memories, and she was the big sister who looked out for him. He had come to them when he escaped prison, and they had looked after him.

"Well, I cannot blame you for standing by your wife," Sir Henry said to Barrymore.

Then Sir Henry and I decided to dress and hunt for the scoundrel on the moor. We knew about where he would be as he waited for the food he expected. I brought my revolver and we headed out.

The night air smelled of damp and decay and an autumn wind moaned. Now and then the moon peeped out of the clouds. We followed the light that still burned to mark the convict waiting for food.

As we walked, we heard the long, rising howl I had heard once before with Stapleton. Then the howl came again. The baronet caught my sleeve and his faced glowed white in the darkness.

"My God, what's that, Watson?" he asked.

"I don't know," I admitted.

We strained our ears in the absolute silence that lay on the moor then. "Watson," the baronet whispered, "it was a hound. I am sure of it." He pointed toward the great Grimpen Mire. "It came from that way."

When we heard nothing else, Sir Henry calmed a bit. We pressed on in pursuit of the convict. We found the candle stuck in a crevice of the rocks to keep the wind from it and to shield the light from all but the Hall. Suddenly, a thin face covered in dirt and a beard peered over the rocks. The light of the candle turned the man's eyes to pits. I had never seen a more savage face.

I sprang forward with Sir Henry but the convict screamed and ran like a mountain goat. I could have brought him down with my revolver, but I had brought it for defense, not to shoot an unarmed man in the back. We chased him for a time but he clearly knew the moor far better than we did.

At one point, the moon broke through the clouds and outlined a man standing on the ridge above us. He was tall and thin and stood with his arms folded and his head bowed. He seemed like the brooding spirit of the place.

I called out to Sir Henry to look but by the time he turned, the man was gone. We searched for the convict for some time but eventually had to turn for home. We solved one mystery to find another. Who was the man on the moor?

CHAPTER
10

The Diary of Dr. Watson

October 16th. A dull, foggy day with a drizzle of rain. I feel danger pressing on us. Twice I have heard the baying of a mysterious hound. The farmers claim to have seen a huge beast with fire shooting out of its mouth and eyes. Holmes would not listen to such tales. Nor should I.

The memory of the stranger on the ridge haunts me. Was this the man who followed Sir Henry in London? I don't speak of my concerns to Sir Henry. Clearly, the sound of the hound on the moor has shaken his nerves.

Barrymore felt we had broken faith with them somehow by chasing the convict. Sir Henry insisted we could not ignore a dangerous man lurking right outside our doors.

"He'll never trouble anyone in the country again," Barrymore said. "I promise. We have made arrangements to send him to South America. Please, let us send him away."

We reluctantly agreed and Barrymore thanked us. Then he added, "You have been so kind, sir. There is something I would tell you about Sir Charles's death. We haven't spoken of it as we want no scandal shadowing Sir Charles. He meant a great deal to us."

"What do you know?" Sir Henry asked.

"I know he was at the gate to meet a woman," Barrymore said. "I don't know her name, but her initials are L. L."

"How do you know this?"

Barrymore told us that Sir Charles had received a letter the morning he died. "Later when my wife was cleaning out the ashes, she found a bit of the letter caught in the grate." Barrymore said. The writer begged Sir Charles to meet her at the gate and to burn the letter.

October 17th. The rain continues to pour, and I almost feel sorry for the convict on the cold, soaking moor. Whenever I think of the moor, I picture again the stranger on the ridge. I walked far on the sodden moor to the ridge where he stood but could find no sign of the mysterious man.

It was on that ramble that I stumbled into Dr. Mortimer. He insisted upon giving me a ride back to the Hall in his cart. As we jolted along the rough road, I asked him if he knew any local woman with the initials L. L.

"Well, I know Laura Lyons," he said thoughtfully. "But she lives in Coombe Tracey. She's the only one."

"Who is she?" I asked.

"She is Frankland's daughter."

This startled me as I could hardly picture Frankland having a daughter. He was so busy with his lawsuits and peeping at the neighbors with his telescope. Dr. Mortimer told me she had married an artist named Lyons. The man deserted her. Her father refused to take her back since she had married without his consent.

I asked how she made a living with no husband and no help from her father. "Sir Charles helped her," the doctor said. "So did Stapleton. They set her up in a typewriting business and I believe she does fairly well."

The only other thing of interest was a discussion between Sir Henry and Barrymore. Sir Henry asked how the convict fared upon the moor.

"I have not heard from him since I set food out three days ago," Barrymore said wearily.

"Did you see him then?" I asked.

"No, but the food was gone when next I went that way, so he must have gotten it. Unless it was taken by the other man on the moor."

I sat bolt upright at that. "You've seen another man?"

Barrymore shook his head. "Selden told me of him, sir. He's in hiding too, but Selden thought he was not a convict. I don't like any of this. I feel certain foul play is brewing."

"What is it that alarms you?" Sir Henry asked.

"Sir Charles's death was bad enough. But now there are howls on the moor at night. Not a man hereabouts would step foot on the moor at night. What does it mean?"

"Did Selden know anything else about the stranger?" I asked.

"Only that he was living in one of the old stone houses on the hillside," Barrymore said. "And that he has a lad who brings him what he needs."

I know that the stranger lies at the heart of all this mystery. I vow not to let another day pass without finding him.

CHAPTER 11

The Man on the Tor

After that diary entry, strange events began to move more swiftly toward their terrible end. I had settled on Laura Lyons and the man on the moor as the focus of my next efforts.

I had no trouble finding the young woman once I reached Coombe Tracey. A maid showed me in without ceremony. I found Laura Lyons sitting before a Remington typewriter.

Mrs. Lyons was beautiful, with hazel eyes and chestnut hair. She asked me the purpose of my visit, and I told her I knew her father. She assured me that she had nothing in common with her father.

"I might have starved for all my father cared," she said. "If it were not for kind hearts like Sir Charles Baskerville, I would have been lost."

"I have come to speak with you about Sir Charles," I said.

The lady went pale, making the freckles on her face stand out. "What can I tell you about him?" she asked.

"Did you correspond with him?" I asked.

She said she had met him only a few times. She wrote to him now and then, mostly to thank him for his help.

Then I told her I knew about the letter she sent on the day of Sir Charles's death. She grew very pale.

"I wished him to help me," she said. "I believed that if he spoke with me, he would."

"Why at such a late hour?" I asked.

"I heard he was going to London the next day," she said. "I felt it was my last chance."

"Why meet him in the garden?"

"I felt it would do my reputation no good to be seen calling on him. I am a young woman alone."

"What happened when you met him there?" I asked.

"I never went."

I pressed her harder, suggesting this information would not look good to the police.

"I wrote the letter because I needed money," she said, nearly crying. "I wanted a divorce, but it would cost more than I had. I wanted my freedom and peace of mind. I believed Sir Charles would help me."

"Then why did you not meet him?"

"I received help from another source."

At that, she stopped all further conversation. I pressed, but she was firm. Finally I left. On my walk home, Mr. Frankland hailed me in the road and told me about the most recent court case he had won.

"Ah," I said. "Then are your days in court at an end for a while?"

"Well, I have learned some interesting information," he said slyly. "Something the police would love to know. It's about the convict on the moor."

I started in surprise, and he launched into a full explanation. He had been watching the moor in his telescope for sight of the convict. He had not seen him, but he had seen the boy who carried his food.

My heart picked up a few beats at that. It wasn't the convict Mr. Frankland had learned about, but the moor stranger.

"It might have been the son of a moor shepherd taking him his dinner," I suggested.

Frankland dragged me over to peer through the telescope at the very route the boy had taken. "There are no shepherds that way," he said. "It's the stoniest part of the whole moor. Your suggestion is silly."

I agreed with him that I was clearly wrong. The old man peered through the telescope again and then yelled. "There's the boy now! Come and see with your own eyes!"

I took my turn at the eyepiece and did see a boy with a bundle on his shoulder. When the boy reached the crest of the hill, he looked around carefully, then continued on. I made my farewells from Mr. Frankland as quickly as I dared and then headed in the direction I had seen the boy.

The sun was already sinking when I crested the hill I had seen the boy upon. Over the wide moor before me, there was no sound and no movement. The boy was nowhere to be seen. I looked over the circle of old stone huts and saw that one had enough roof still to offer some shelter. My heart leaped when I saw it. This must be where the stranger lurked.

The place was empty, but I found blankets upon the stone slab that had served as a bed. Ashes lay in the grate and some cooking utensils were set close at hand. A little bundle held bread and cans of peaches. It also contained a note: "Dr. Watson has gone to Coombe Tracey."

This stranger was tracking my movements. I must say that set on my heart heavily. I slipped out of the hut and hid nearby to wait on the stranger. Finally, I heard his boot steps on the rocky ground. I crouched in the dark, my pistol in my hand.

"It is a lovely evening, my dear Watson," a well-known voice said.

CHAPTER 12

Death on the Moor

"Holmes!" I cried.

"Come out," he said. "And do be careful with your gun."

I slipped out from behind the rocks and looked into his gray eyes, dancing with amusement. His clothes were neat and he was even clean shaven! Only Holmes could live rough in the wild and still look the same as on any day on Baker Street.

"I was never more glad to see anyone in my life," I said as I shook his hand. "This mystery has been very hard on my nerves."

I admitted that I had not guessed the moor stranger could be him. He admitted he had no idea I had found his hiding place until he was practically on top of me. He quizzed me on how I had found him and I proudly gave the details.

"You didn't trust me," I said finally. "You let me think I was alone here."

"You might have led to my discovery," he said. "You would have wished to tell me something or to bring me some comfort or another. You're a very kindhearted man. As it was, I had Cartwright to look after me."

"So my reports were for nothing," I said, and my voice actually cracked.

"Your reports have been invaluable," he said. "They have given me a different perspective. And you have been far closer to Sir Henry than I. Now tell me about Laura Lyons."

I told him what I had learned on my visit.

"That fills in a gap in this complex affair. I knew the lady was involved with the man Stapleton. Now, if I could use that knowledge to turn Stapleton's wife to our side."

"His wife?"

"The lady he claims as his sister is really his wife," Holmes said solemnly.

"How could he have permitted Sir Henry to fall in love with her?"

"He knew it could do no harm to anyone except Sir Henry," Holmes said. "And I believe he means him harm enough."

"So Stapleton followed Sir Henry in London?" I said. "And the warning came from her? She has warned him since as well, but I did not make the connection. How can you be sure?"

"He told you that he was a schoolmaster in the north," Holmes said. "That made him easy to track. He lived there with his wife until a scandal hit the school and he disappeared."

"Then where does Laura Lyons come in?" I asked.

"She believes him to be an unmarried man with a sister," Holmes said. "So he won her heart and pressed her to get a divorce so he could marry her. I am certain it was Stapleton who put the idea in her head of getting money from Sir Charles."

"When she learns the truth . . .," I whispered.

"She may wish to help us," Holmes finished.

"But what is all this deception for?" I asked.

"Murder, Watson. My net is closing in on him even as his closes in on Sir Henry. With your help, we shall have him. Until then, you must guard Sir Henry closely."

Just then, we heard a scream of horror and pain. The fear in the sound turned the blood to ice in my veins. We heard more shouts and a deep rumble as well.

"The hound," Holmes cried. "Come, Watson. We may already be too late!"

Holmes ran swiftly over the moor and I followed at his heels. We heard one last despairing yell and then a dull heavy thud.

"He has beaten us, Watson," Holmes moaned. "We are too late."

We ran blindly through the gloom, then finally we caught a low moan to our left. On that side, a ridge of rock ended in a sheer cliff. A man lay facedown on the slope below. I recognized the clothes in a moment and knew it was Sir Henry Baskerville.

"Oh, Holmes!" I cried with clenched hands. "I shall never forgive myself for having left him alone."

We scrambled down the hill to retrieve our friend's body. Suddenly Holmes jumped up and yelled. "A beard! This man has a beard! It is my neighbor, the convict!"

I realized Barrymore must have given these clothes to his brother-in-law. Everything he wore had been Sir Henry's. "I am amazed a man like this would be afraid of a dog on the moor," I said.

"The greater question is why the hound was loose tonight," Holmes said.

Then as we stood by the body, we heard approaching footsteps. It was Stapleton.

"Hello, Dr. Watson," he said. "Is someone hurt? Oh no, is that our friend Sir Henry?"

"No," I said. "It is Selden, the man who escaped from Princetown."

Stapleton turned a ghastly pale face upon us, but then looked sharply at Holmes. "How shocking. How did he die?"

"He seems to have fallen," Holmes said. "We were walking and heard the cry."

"I heard it as well and worried it might be Sir Henry," Stapleton said. "He had said he would come over but when he didn't come, I was worried. I am so glad it wasn't our friend. What do make of this, Mr. Holmes?"

"You are quick at identification," Holmes said.

"I have been expecting you since Dr. Watson arrived," Stapleton replied.

Holmes nodded. "I must return to London tomorrow though. This has not been a satisfactory case. I have little interest in legends and rumors."

Holmes sounded so unconcerned that I nearly gaped at him. We dealt quickly with the body. Then Holmes and I set off to Baskerville Hall, leaving Stapleton to return to his home alone.

CHAPTER 13

Fixing the Nets

"What nerve that fellow has," Holmes said as we walked across the moor.

"I am sorry he has seen you."

Holmes waved that away. "There is no getting out of it. Like most clever men, I am certain he feels he has tricked us."

"I would like to arrest him at once!"

"Spoken as a true man of action," Holmes said with a laugh. "Let's build a case first with evidence. We have to prove his hand in this. Even tonight we have no clear connection between the hound and the man's death."

"So how do we make our case?" I asked.

"I have great hopes for what Mrs. Lyons may do when she learns about Mrs. Stapleton. I have a plan of my own as well, but that is for tomorrow. Until then, say nothing of the hound to Sir Henry."

Sir Henry was delighted to see Sherlock Holmes. I had the unpleasant duty of breaking the news of Selden to Barrymore and his wife. She wept bitterly in her apron, but I suspect Barrymore felt great relief to have it over.

Over a late dinner, Sir Henry said, "Stapleton invited me over. But I did not go out on the moor without you, even though it would have made for a more lively evening."

"Yes, it would have been a lively evening," Holmes said dryly. "But you should know we had a touching moment of mourning over you."

"How is that?" Sir Henry said.

"The convict was wearing your clothes. I assume Barrymore had dressed him for his new life in South America."

"Watson and I have not had much luck with our deductions on this case," Sir Henry said. "I do know there is a dog on the moor somewhere. I've heard it."

"I believe we can muzzle and chain him with your help," Holmes said.

"Whatever you ask me to do, I'll do it," Sir Henry agreed.

"I may ask you to do it blindly, without question or hesitation."

"Just as you like."

Suddenly Holmes's attention was drawn to a portrait of a man in black velvet and lace. He stared at it fixedly, then asked about it.

"That is the wicked Hugo who brought the curse upon us," Sir Henry said. "The portraits are all Baskervilles of some sort. Barrymore has been schooling me in them."

"He looks like such a quiet, mild-mannered man," Holmes said. He said nothing more about the painting, but I saw his eyes turn to it several more times in the evening. After Sir Henry retired for the evening, I asked Holmes about his interest.

Holmes climbed up on a chair and held up the light in his left hand while using his arm to cover the hat and ringlets. The face of Stapleton sprang out of the canvas.

"That is amazing," I said. "It could have been his portrait."

"It is evident the fellow is a Baskerville," Holmes said. "And that suggests a motive for these killings. By tomorrow night, he will be fluttering in our net like one of his butterflies."

Holmes rose early the next morning and sent a report to the police on the death of Selden. He also let Cartwright know where he was. Over breakfast, Holmes turned to Sir Henry and said, "You are to dine with the Stapletons tonight?"

"I am."

"Good. Watson and I must go to London but you should keep that dinner appointment. I wish you to drive to Merripit House for dinner, then send back your trap and tell the Stapletons you intend to walk home."

Sir Henry looked alarmed. "Walk across the moor?"

"Yes," Holmes said calmly.

"You told me I must not ever walk on the moor at night," Sir Henry prodded.

"Tonight, you should. Walk along the straight path from Merripit House to the Grimpen Road. It is important."

"I will do just as you say."

"Good, then Watson and I must leave at once," Holmes said as he rose from his chair.

I was no more comfortable with the plan than Sir Henry, but I went along with Holmes. We met up with Cartwright at the station in Coombe Tracey. Holmes told Cartwright to run to the station office and see if there was a wire from Inspector Lestrade. Cartwright quickly returned with a telegram. The inspector was coming with an unsigned warrant.

"Good," Holmes said. "We may need his assistance. Now, let us pass the time by calling upon Mrs. Lyons."

The change in Mrs. Lyons upon learning Stapleton had a wife was impressive. Holmes produced proof in the form of a photo and papers from Stapleton's time as a schoolmaster. Her face grew gray as she looked over the papers.

"He said he would marry me as soon as I was divorced from Lyons," she whispered. Then she looked up fiercely. "He told me to send the letter to Sir Charles. He dictated it. And he convinced me not to go to the meeting."

Holmes nodded as she confirmed what he knew. We left Mrs. Lyons and headed to the station to meet the London express. A wiry bulldog of a man sprang from the first-class carriage. We all shook hands, and I was pleased to see the warmth with which Lestrade greeted Holmes. They had not always been on such good terms.

"This is the biggest case you'll see for years," Holmes said. "We shall eat dinner and then we'll take a breath of night air on the moor. I promise you won't forget your visit."

The Hound of the Baskervilles

One of the most frustrating traits of my good friend Sherlock Holmes is that he does not like to give details of his plans until they are sprung. I must admit, the long day did nothing positive for my nerves. I felt amazing relief once I knew we were drawing near the Hall and the scene of the action.

Holmes called to the driver to stop near the gate of the avenue. Then, we started to walk to Merripit House in the dark.

"Are you armed, Lestrade?" Holmes asked.

The little detective smiled. "If I have trousers, you can be sure I have a little something in my hip pocket."

"Good," Holmes said. "Then we are all well prepared for emergencies. Now we must play a waiting game."

When we drew close to Merripit House, Holmes cautioned us to walk softly and speak in rare whispers. We halted about 200 yards from the house and crouched behind some rocks.

From there we could see into the window that shone brightly from the dining room. The blinds were up and Holmes instructed me to creep close and see what was going on inside.

I saw Sir Henry and Stapleton alone in the room. They sat on either side of the round table and seemed to be talking amiably. I noticed the baronet looked a bit on edge.

Suddenly Stapleton left the room, and I heard the creak of an outside door and boots on gravel. He walked to a building at the corner of the orchard. I heard a key turn in a lock and a curious scuffling sound. Then Stapleton returned to the house.

I crept quietly back to my companions and reported. "You say the lady was not there?" Holmes asked. He seemed concerned by that but said nothing more.

A dense, white fog hung over the Grimpen Mire. It was drifting slowly in our direction like a shimmering wall. Holmes looked at the creeping whiteness and muttered impatiently, "Sir Henry must come out before the fog."

Every minute the thick fog drifted closer and closer to the house. When the fog finally covered us, Holmes said, "I think I hear him coming."

A quick sound of steps broke the silence of the moor. The steps grew louder and louder through the fog. Sir Henry moved swiftly along the path, passing close to where we lay. As he walked, he glanced often behind him. Then he disappeared again into the fog.

"Look out!" cried Holmes, and I heard the sharp click of his pistol as he cocked it. "It's coming!"

There was a thin, crisp patter from somewhere in the heart of the fog. All three of us stared into the wall of white, uncertain of what horror was about to appear.

I glanced at Holmes and saw his eyes shining brightly in the moonlight. Then his lips parted in amazement. At the same second, Lestrade gave a yell of terror. I sprang to my feet, my mind stunned senseless by the dreadful shape that bolted from the darkness.

It was an enormous, coal-black hound. Fire burst from its open mouth, and its eyes glowed with a smoldering glare. We were so stunned by the sight that we let the hound pass before we fired. The creature gave a hideous howl but did not pause.

We raced after it and saw Sir Henry looking back, his face white in the moonlight. He raised his hands in horror as the beast rushed at him.

Sir Henry screamed. The hound roared. I saw it spring at Sir Henry and hurl him to the ground.

In the next instant, Holmes had emptied his revolver into the creature. The beast howled in agony, snapped at us, and then dropped to the ground. The giant hound was dead. We bent over Sir Henry and found no sign of a wound.

"What was it?" he gasped. "What was it?"

"It's dead, whatever it was," Holmes said.

The animal seemed to be a mix of mastiff and bloodhound and was incredibly large. I touched the glow on the creature's muzzle, and my fingers came away gleaming in the darkness.

"Phosphorus," I said.

"I am sorry, Sir Henry," Holmes said. "We should not have let the creature get so close."

"You saved my life."

"After first risking it. Are you strong enough that we might leave you? We have another murderer to capture. Those shots must have warned him, but we might catch him yet."

We retraced our path swiftly. The front door stood open, so we rushed in. The elderly manservant simply gawked at us as we dashed through the house. Holmes grabbed the lamp from the dining room and led the way.

On the upper floor, we found a locked room. A faint moaning and rustling came from within. Holmes kicked the door just above the lock and it flew open. Pistols in hand, we rushed into the room.

The walls were lined with glass-topped cases full of dead butterflies and moths pinned to black velvet. In the center of the room, a figure stood lashed to an upright beam.

The figure was so wrapped in sheets that all we could see were two dark eyes. We tore off the wrappings and Mrs. Stapleton sank to the floor, her head bowed. The mark of a whiplash was clear on her neck.

"The brute!" Holmes cried as we lifted her into a chair.

"Is he safe?" she gasped. "Has he escaped?"

"He cannot escape us, madam," Holmes said coldly.

"No, no, I don't mean my husband. Is Sir Henry safe?" Mrs. Stapleton asked.

"Yes," Holmes replied.

"And the hound?"

"Dead."

Mrs. Stapleton gave a long sigh of satisfaction. She told us she was certain Stapleton would head for the mire.

"There is an old tin mine on the island in the heart of the mire," she said. "He kept the hound there. That is where he would go in a time of trouble," she said.

Holmes looked out at the white wall of fog. "No one could find their way in the Grimpen Mire tonight."

"He uses marks to show him the way," she said as she turned toward the window. "But he would have to see them to make the way safely."

Lestrade stayed behind as we took Sir Henry home. The shock of the night's adventures brought on a fever, and he spent weeks under the care of Dr. Mortimer. The two of them would travel the world before Sir Henry became the hearty man he'd been before.

The next day, Mrs. Stapleton took us along the trail through the bog. The mud sucked at our heels as we walked. When we found the mine, Holmes cried aloud and seized an old black boot that lay in the mud. "Stapleton used this to set the hound on Sir Henry's scent."

We found signs of the dog. There were tufts of hair and gnawed bones. Nearby a tin lay in the dirt.

"This paste in the tin is no doubt the luminous mixture he used on the dog," Holmes said. "I do believe this is the most dangerous man we've ever chased. And one we'll never catch, for I believe the mire caught him first."

Holmes swept his long arm toward the huge, mottled expanse of green-splotched bog. It stretched away until it merged into the russet slopes of the moor.

CHAPTER
15

A Retrospective

On a night at the end of November, Holmes and I sat on either side of a blazing fire in our sitting room on Baker Street. Sir Henry and Dr. Mortimer had stopped by on their way to that long voyage that would mend Sir Henry's shattered nerves.

"Do you have all the facts you need to write up the case?" Holmes asked.

"Perhaps one or two might be added," I said. "How did Stapleton come to look so much like Hugo?"

"He was the son of Rodger Baskerville, the younger brother of Sir Charles. Rodger had fled to South America to avoid scandal and possible legal problems. He died there, but not before fathering a son.

"The young man married Beryl Garcia and proceeded to steal a great deal of money and flee to England. He established that school in Yorkshire, but the school fell pray to scandal. It was then that he changed his name to Stapleton and came to Devonshire."

"Where he intended to kill Sir Charles?" I said.

"Clearly," Holmes agreed. "Though it was Sir Charles who put the tools in his hand by telling him about the hound, which the old man had feared all his life. The timing for the death came from Dr. Mortimer's suggestion that Sir Charles spend some time away for the sake of his nerves."

"And for that, Stapleton used Mrs. Lyons," I said.

"Only because Mrs. Stapleton refused to play a part in the old man's death," Holmes said. "But it was certainly Stapleton who sent the hound over the moor gate to chase Sir Charles to his death. If he had stopped there, it would have been nearly impossible to ever find him guilty of murder."

"But Sir Henry came," I said.

"Yes, and I suspect that was a surprise to Stapleton. I doubt he knew of another heir. He tracked Sir Henry in London and stole the boot to use in a repeat performance of the hound."

"But his wife sent messages of warning," I said. "First the note, then speaking directly to me and later to Sir Henry. But who cared for the hound when Stapleton was in London?"

"The old manservant," Holmes said. "He disappeared the morning after Sir Henry's near death. I've looked into his background and he had been with Stapleton for many years— possibly all the way back to South America."

"Stapleton couldn't have expected a young man like Sir Henry would simply drop dead of fear," I said.

"The beast was savage and half-starved," Holmes said. "If it didn't frighten him to death, it would certainly hold him viciously until Stapleton could creep close enough to finish the job."

"But how could that benefit Stapleton?" I asked. "He could hardly pretend to suddenly remember he was an heir."

"I do not know that part of the plan," Holmes said. "Perhaps he planned a disguise. Or maybe he intended to return to South America and make his claim from there with proof of his relation to Rodger. I don't doubt he had a plan. He was a worthy foe, Watson. He makes me wonder who we might encounter next."